# MARRYING
# DAMIAN

# MARRYING
# DAMIAN

WILLIAM TREVOR

COLOPHON PRESS

1995

Published by Colophon Press
18a Prentis Road London SW16 1QD

© William Trevor 1994

The author has asserted his moral right
to be identified as the author of this work.

Numbered copies ISBN 1 874122 18 0
Lettered copies ISBN 1 874122 19 9

A CIP Catalogue record for this book
is available from the British Library

Set in 14 point Fournier
and printed by letterpress at
Libanus Press Ltd, Marlborough
Bound by The Fine Bindery
Wellingborough

*For James Michie*

'I'm going to marry Damian,' Joanna said.

Claire wasn't paying attention. She smiled and nodded, intent on unravelling a ball of garden twine that had become tangled. I said:

'Well, that's nice of course. But Damian's married already.'

It didn't matter, Joanna said, and repeated her resolve. Joanna was five at the time.

\*

Twenty-two years later Damian stood on the wild grass, among the cornflowers and the echiums and the lavatera, under the cricket-bat willow that had been a two-foot shrub when Joanna made her announcement. He was wearing blue sunglasses and a powder-blue suit that looked new. In contrast, his tie – its maroon and gold stripes seeming to indicate membership of some club to which almost certainly Damian did not belong – was lank, and the collar of his shirt was frayed. We hadn't been expecting him; we hadn't heard from Damian for years. Since the spring of 1985, Claire afterwards calculated, the year after his second divorce, from an American widow in upstate New York. Before that there had been an English woman who lived in Venice, about whom we had never been told very much. When Joanna had declared her childhood intention Damian had been still married to the only one of his three wives Claire and I actually knew: a slender, pretty girl, the daughter of the Bishop of Killaloe. We had known her since the wedding; I'd been Damian's best man.

I was actually asleep when Damian walked into our garden all those years later, and I think Claire was too. We were lolling in deckchairs, Claire's spaniels stretched out under hers, avoiding the afternoon sun.

'Yes,' Damian said. 'It's Damian.'

We were surprised, but perhaps not much: turning up out of the blue had always been his style. He never telephoned first or intimated his intention by letter or on a postcard. Over the years he had arrived in all seasons and at varying times of day, once rousing us at two o'clock in the morning. Invariably he brought with him details of a personal disaster which had left him with the need to borrow a little money. These loans were not paid back; even as he accepted them he made no pretence that they would be.

'Damian.' Claire hugged him, laughing, playfully demanding to know what he was doing in that awful suit. I asked him where he'd been and he said oh, a lot of places – Vancouver, Oregon, Spain. Claire made him sit down, saying she was going to make some tea, inviting him to stay a while. He was the tonic we needed, Claire said, for she's always afraid that we'll slump into dullness unless we're careful. A woman, somewhere, had given him the suit: we both guessed that.

'I wasn't all that well in Spain,' Damian said. 'Some kind of sunstroke.'

We are the same age, Damian and I, not young any more: that day, as we sat together in the garden, we were sixty and a bit, Claire five years younger. She's tall and slim, and I can't believe she'll ever be anything but elegant, but of course I know I may be wrong. When we married she came to live in the country town I've always known, acquiring an extra identity as the doctor's wife and the receptionist at the practice, as the mother of a daughter and a son, the organiser of a playgroup, the woman who first taught the illiterate of the town to read.

Damian, at the first opportunity, fled this neighbourhood. On his return to it the time before this one he had carried – clearly an affectation – a silver-topped cane, which was abandoned now, no doubt because it drew attention to its own necessity, and Damian inclines towards vanity. Although he sat down briskly in the chair Claire had vacated for him, the protest of a joint caused him, for a

8

single instant, to wince. His light, fair hair is grey in places now, and I don't suppose he cares for that either, or that his teeth have shrivelled and become discoloured, nor that the freckles on the backs of his hands form blobs where they have spread into one another, nor that the skin of his forehead is as dry as old vellum. But that day there was nothing about his eyes to suggest a coming to terms with a future destined to be different from the past, no hint of a hesitation about what should or should not be undertaken: in that sense Damian remains young.

Even as a boy his features were gaunt, giving the impression then of under-nourishment. He was angular, but without any of the awkwardness sometimes associated with that quality. In spite of whatever trouble he was having with a joint, he could still, I noticed that day, tidy himself away with natural ease. As always at the beginning of a visit, he was good-humoured; moodiness – sometimes a snappish response to questions, or silence – was apt to set in later.

If, in terms of having a profession, Damian is anything, he is a poet, although in all the time I've known him he has never shown me more than a verse or two. Years ago someone told us that he once had a coterie of admirers and was still, in certain quarters, considered to possess 'a voice' that should be more widely heard. A volume entitled 'Slow Death of a Pigeon' – its contents sparse, Claire and I always assumed, for nothing about Damian suggests he is profligate with his talent – appears to represent all he has so far chosen for posterity. In time we would receive a copy of 'Slow Death of a Pigeon', he promised on one of his visits, but none arrived.

'Well, yes, it was that. Something like it,' he was saying, slightly laughing, when I returned with another deckchair after Claire had brought out the tea things. He had repeated all he'd told me about his sunstroke and the lack of anything of interest in Vancouver. Yes, he was confessing now, a relationship with a woman had featured in his more recent travels, had somehow been the reason for them.

9

There was no confirmation that the powder-blue suit had been a gift. Damian wouldn't have considered that of interest.

'I thought I'd maybe die,' he said, returning to the subject of his sunstroke, but when I asked him what he'd taken for it, what treatment there had been, he was vague.

'Bloody visions,' he said instead. 'Goya stuff.' In any case, he confidently pronounced, Spain was over-rated.

Had the woman been Spanish? I wondered, and thought of dancers, white teeth and a rosebud that was red, black skirts swirling, red ribbons in black hair. I have doctor colleagues who farm a bit, who let the wind blow away the mixture of triviality and death that now and again makes our consulting rooms melancholy places. Others collect rare books, make cabinets, involve themselves in politics, allow gardening or some sport to become a way of life to skulk in. For me, Damian's infrequent visits, and wondering about him in between, were such a diversion. Not as efficacious as afternoons on a tractor or searching out a Cuala Press edition of Yeats, but then by nature I'm lazy.

'A chapter closed?' Claire was saying.

'Should never have been opened.'

Later, in the kitchen, I decanted the wine and Claire said the lamb would be enough, with extra potatoes and courgettes. We heard Joanna's car and then her voice exclaiming in surprise and Damian greeting her.

I carried a tray of drinks to the garden. Damian's small black suitcase, familiar to us for many years, was still on the grass beside his deckchair. I can see it now.

*

The visit followed a familiar pattern. In the small suitcase there were shirts and underclothes and socks in need of laundering; and when they had been through the washing-machine most of them were seen to be in need of repair. Damian, besides, was penniless; and there was the request that if anyone telephoned him – which was, he said, unlikely since, strictly speaking, no one knew his whereabouts – his presence in our house should be denied.

When we were children, Damian and I had played together at Doul, the grey, half-derelict house where his Aunt Una had brought him up. Doul is no longer there, having been sold to a builder for the lead of its roof, and later razed to the ground. Damian's Aunt Una had drunk herself to death in a caravan. I was actually there when her head jerked suddenly to one side on the pillow, the visible indication of her demise. She'd been, in our childhood, a vague presence in that old house and its lost garden, tall and handsome yet somehow like a ghost of someone else: it was said that she was Damian's mother. People who remembered her advent, with an infant, in the neighbourhood, said the house had been bought for her by the man who'd made her pregnant, buying her silence also.

I learned all that later. When Damian and I were eight his Aunt Una was known to me as his aunt and there was never a reason, afterwards, to doubt that she was. He and I were sent away to different schools – the seducer from the past said to have obliged in this way, also, where Damian's boarding fees were concerned – but our friendship none the less continued. Damian – like a scarecrow sometimes because it was never noticed by his Aunt Una that he grew out of his clothes – was easy company, hard to dislike, an antidote to the provincial respectability I grew up in. We wandered about the countryside; we hung about point-to-points; when we were older we went to Friday dancehalls if one of us had money; we dreamed of romance with Bettina Nowd, clerk in the Munster and Leinster Bank. Abruptly, our ways parted, and remained so for a long time: when Damian, at nineteen, left the neighbourhood he did not return for fourteen years, by which time his Aunt Una was dead and her house gone. It was said he hadn't written to her, or communicated in any way during that time, which was surprising because he was always fond of her. But as I heard nothing from him either it's perhaps less odd than it seems. For Damian, perhaps, the vacuum of people's absence cannot be filled by any other means. During that fourteen years he and I met only once, at Killaloe at the first of his weddings.

'You know, I'd like to see Doul again,' he said the day after he'd appeared in his powder-blue suit. So we went there, where there was nothing to see, not even the caravan his Aunt Una died in. Beneath the brambles that grew everywhere, and the great swathes of nettles, there might have been remains of some kind, but if there were the naked eye could not discern them. When we walked on a bit there were the walls of the kitchen garden, ivy-clad in places, fallen away in others.

'You couldn't build Doul again,' I pointed out when he said he'd like to. 'Not without a fortune, Damian.'

He muttered, and for the first time sounded disagreeable. There was some kind of complaint, a protest about his continuing lack of means, and then: 'The avenue . . . the gates . . .'

A fragment from a poem? I wondered. Sometimes in Damian's conversation words stand isolated and out of context, as though they do not belong in conversation at all.

'The house,' I began.

'Oh, not the house as it was.'

Claire's spaniels sniffed about for rabbits. As we stood there, the September sun felt hot. Damian believes in the impossible and when we were younger occasionally inspired me with his optimism: that nothing could be easier than poaching salmon, that a bookie or a publican would accept an I.O.U., that Bettina Nowd had the love-light in her eyes. It was an endearing quality then; I wasn't so sure about it being one that had endearingly endured. I felt uneasy about this talk of coming back. During the companionship of our youth there had never been an attempt to borrow money since there was none to lend; nor was advantage taken of small politenesses since politeness was not then readily on offer. The threat of a neighbour with a fly-by-night's presumptions was just a little alarming.

'Who owns it now?' he asked, and I told him: the son of the builder who had stripped the roof of its lead.

The cawing of rooks and the occasional bark of the dogs were the only sounds. It had always been quiet at Doul; that tall, beautiful woman floating about from room to room or picking the last of the mulberries; bees in the honeysuckle.

'What?' I said, again unable to catch Damian's murmur. Still moody, he did not directly reply, but seemed to say that the Muse would not be silent here.

*

I had ceased to practise on my sixtieth birthday, feeling the time had come, although previously I had imagined I could go on more or less for ever, as my father had in this same house, to his dying day. 'What'll it be like?' Damian used to ponder when we were young, the world for him an excitement to investigate, after a small, familiar town in southwest Ireland. Both of us, of course, knew what it would be like for me: we knew my father's house, its comfortably crowded rooms, its pleasant garden; we knew the narrow main street, the shopkeepers, priests, and beggars, the condensed-milk factory, the burnt-out cinema, the sleepy courthouse, the bright new hospital, the old asylum, the prison. But neither of us could conjecture a single thing about what lay ahead for Damian.

'It's all right, is it?' Damian asked me on the way back from Doul that day, his mood gregarious again, suddenly so, as if he had remembered who I was. 'Doing nothing these days is all right?'

'Yes, it's all right.'

In fact, it was more than that: all sorts of things were easier in retirement. People weren't patients any more. Met by chance on the street, they conversed with less embarrassment; while privately I registered that Raynaud's was at work or that Frolich's Syndrome would not now be reversed. In ordinary chat, awkward secrets were not shared with me; more likely I was shown an adolescent's face and then reminded I'd been the first to see it as an infant's; or informed of athletic achievements in children who had grown up, or of success in other ways, and weddings that were planned. Worries were held back, not coinage for me now, as bad backs weren't, or stitched wounds or blood pressure, the smell of sickness in small back bedrooms.

'Yes, it's fine' I said in the bar of Traynor's Hotel. 'And you?' I added. 'Nowadays, Damian?'

Again he became morose. He shrugged and did not answer. He stared at the back of a man who was standing at the bar, at the torn seam of a jacket. Then he said:

'I used to think about Doul. Wherever I was, I'd come back to that.'

From his tone, those thoughts about the place of his youth had been a comfort, occurring – the implication was – at times of distress or melancholy. Then Damian said, as if in response to a question I had not asked:

'Well yes, an inspiration.'

He had finished the whiskey in his glass. I went to the bar, and while the drinks I ordered were poured I was asked by Mr Traynor about our son, now a doctor in New South Wales, and about Joanna, who had returned to the town six months ago to work in the prison. 'You'd be delighted she's back here,' Mr Traynor conjectured, and I agreed, although pointing out that sooner or later she would move away again. I smiled, shrugging that away, my mind not on the conversation. Could Doul have been a poet's inspiration for all these years? I wondered. Was that the meaning I was supposed to find in what had been so vaguely stated?

'I thought I recognised him,' Mr Traynor next remarked, his voice kept low, after I had answered his query about who Damian was. 'How're you doing these times?' he called out, and Damian called back that none of us was getting younger.

'God, that's the truth in it,' Mr Traynor agreed, wagging his head in a pretence that this hadn't occurred to him before.

I picked up my change and made my way back to the table where we sat.

'Nothing grand,' Damian said, as if my absence hadn't interrupted what we'd been saying. 'Any little hovel that could be knocked together. There're things . . .' He let the sentence trail away. 'I have the time now.'

I sipped my drink, disguising amusement: all his life Damian had had time. He ran through time, spending it as a spendthrift, wallowing in idleness. Perhaps poets always did, perhaps it was the way they had to live; I didn't know.

'Stuff accumulates,' Damian confided, 'unsaid. Oh, it's just a thought,' he added, and I concluded, with considerable relief, that this was probably the last we'd hear of his morning's whim. After all, there was no sign whatsoever of his being in possession of the necessary funds to build the modest dwelling he spoke of, and personal loans could be resisted. 'Silly old Damian,' Claire murmured when I told her, with the indulgent smile that talk of Damian always drew from her.

*

Then, quite suddenly, everything was different. Perhaps in the same moment – at dinner two days later – Claire and I were aware that our daughter was being charmed all over again by the man she had once picked out as the man she would like to marry. To this day, I can hear their two voices in my dining-room, and Damian laughing while Claire and I were numbed into silence. To this day I can see the bright flush in Joanna's cheeks.

'And are you settled, Joanna?' Damian asked. 'Here?'

'For the time being,' Joanna said.

The prison is two miles outside the town, a conglomeration of stark grey buildings behind high grey walls, which occasionally I have visited during an epidemic. *Ad sum ard labor*, a waggish inmate has carved on a sundial he made for the governor, a tag that is a talking point when visitors are led around. Joanna has worked in prisons in Dublin and in England; she came here because from conversations she has had with me she was aware that rehabilitation – which is her territory – wasn't being much bothered with. It was a challenge that here on the doorstep of the town she was born and grew up in were circumstances that professionally outraged her.

'I remember sharing a railway carriage with a man who'd just been released from gaol,' Damian said. 'He robbed garages.'

In Joanna's view a spell in prison was the offer of another chance for an offender, a time to come to terms with the world and with oneself. She was an optimist; you had to be, she insisted.

'Lonely wayside garages,' Damian said. 'A child working the pumps.'

'Did he say –'

'All he said was that he didn't intend to get caught the next time.'

Beneath these exchanges there was something else, a tremor that was shared; a tick answered another tick, fingers touched although a dinner-table separated them. I pushed my knife and fork together; and Claire said something that nobody heard and went to the kitchen.

Joanna is small and dark-haired, and pretty. She has had admirers, a proposal of marriage from a map-maker, a longish affair with an ornithologist, but her passionate devotion to her work has always seemed to make her draw back when there was pressure that a relationship should be allowed the assumption of permanence. It was as though she protected her own dedication, as though she believed she would experience a disloyalty in herself if she in any way devoted less time and energy to her work. Recidivists, penitents, old lags, one-time defaulters, drug pushers, muggers, burglars, rapists: these were her lovers. She found the good in them, and yet, when telling us about them, did not demand that we should too. It has never been her way to lecture, or stridently to insist, and often people are surprised at the intensity of her involvement, at the steel beneath so soft a surface. Neither Claire nor I ever say so, but there is something in our daughter that is remarkable.

Across the dinner table that evening she became demure. There was obedience in her glance, and respect for every ordinary word our visitor uttered, as though she would blindly have acted as he dictated should his next words express a desire. I followed Claire into the kitchen, carrying plates and dishes. 'I always wanted to,' Joanna was saying, drawn out by Damian in a way that was not usual in his conversation. 'I never thought of doing anything else.'

We didn't speak, Claire and I, in the kitchen. We didn't even look at one another. It was our fault; we had permitted this stroke of fate to stake its claim. The suitable admirers – the dark-haired map-maker, the ornithologist, and others – were not what a retriever of lost causes, a daily champion of down-and-outs, had ever wanted. In the dining-room the voices chatted on, and in the kitchen we felt invaded by them, Claire and I, she tumbling raspberries into a blue glass bowl, I spooning coffee into the filter. 'I remember hearing you'd been born,' Damian was saying in the dining-room when we returned.

It was I who had told him. I delivered Joanna myself; Claire and I heard her first cry in the same moment. 'A girl,' I said when Damian arrived six months later for one of his visits, and we drank my whiskey on a bitter January night. 'How nice to have a daughter!'

he murmured when we gazed down at the cot by Claire's bedside. And he was right: it was nice having a girl as well as a boy, nice being a family. Even then, two different personalities were apparent: our son's easy-going, rarely ruffled, Joanna's confident. At five and six, long-legged and determined, she won the races she ran because insistently she believed she could. Oh no, she wouldn't, she asserted when it was pointed out that she would tire of looking after the unattractive terrier she rescued after tinkers left it behind. And for years, until the creature died in old age, she did look after it.

'It was snowing outside,' Damian reminisced in the dining-room. 'Black Bush was what we drank, Joanna, the night your father and I wet the baby's head.'

His fingernails were rimmed: ash from the cigarettes he was smoking, as he always does, between courses. Once upon a time, years ago, he affected a cigarette-holder. He had sold it, he told Claire when she asked, and we guessed it had been another gift from a woman, sold when the affair was over.

'Raspberries, Damian?' Claire offered.

He smiled his acceptance. He placed his cigarette, still burning, on a side plate, and poured cream on the fruit. I wondered if children had been born to him; I hadn't wondered that before. I imagined, as I often had, his public-house life in London, some places he could not enter because of debts, late-night disagreements turning sour. I had a feeling that his travels to other places – so often mentioned – had always been of brief duration, that London was where he had mostly belonged, in seedy circumstances. I imagined lodgings, rent unpaid, possessions pawned. How often had there been flits in the small hours? Were small dishonesties a poet's right? And yet, I thought as well, he was our friend and almost always had been. He'd cheered our lives.

'Damian's tired of London,' Joanna said. 'He's going to live at Doul again.'

*

In the night, believing me to be asleep, Claire wept. I whispered, trying to console her. We didn't say to one another that shock came into this, that we must allow a little time to calm us. We lay there, remembering that not much longer than twenty-four hours ago Claire had said our friend was the tonic we needed. On all his visits we'd never been dismayed to see him, and he couldn't help being older now, less handsome than he had been, his grubbiness more noticeable. He was, at heart, as he had always been. It was unfair to say he wasn't, just because he had cast a spell in our house. We'd always known about those spells. We'd read between the lines, we hadn't been misled.

Marriage was what we dreaded, although neither of us used the word. It was not because Damian had so often confessed he liked to marry that our melancholy threw up this stark prediction; it was because Joanna was Joanna. We might be wrong, we felt each other thinking; a tawdry love affair might be enough. But we did not believe it and neither of us suggested the consolation of this lesser pain. Nor did we remind one another that Joanna, all her life, had been attracted by the difficult, nor did we share it with one another when in the dark we were more certainly aware that there had been no challenge in her relationship with the map-maker or the ornithologist, or with any of her suitable admirers. Perhaps, that night, we knew our daughter a little better, and perhaps we loved her just a little more. She would succeed where other women had failed: already we could hear her offering this, already we sensed her not believing that the failure could lie anywhere but with those other women. 'I'm going to marry Damian,' the childish silliness brightly echoed, and with it our amusement.

Had he come to us this time with a purpose? Claire asked when she ceased to weep. Did he intend our daughter to earn his living for him, to tend him in the place of his childhood, cosseting his old man's frailties? Had his future lit up suddenly on a London street, the years ahead radiant as a jewel in his imagination? 'I'll tell them,' had our daughter said already, planning to sit us down, to pour out drinks in celebration? She would break the news that was not news, and we'd embrace her, not pointing out that Damian couldn't help destroying his achievements. And she would hurry to him when he next appeared and they would stand together as lovers do. We could not foretell the details after that, and quite suddenly the form the relationship might take in time hardly seemed to matter any more: enough of it was there already. 'Are we being punished?' Claire asked, and I didn't know if we were or not, or why we should be punished, or what our sin was.

We didn't want that night to end. We didn't want to feel, again, the excitement that had crept into our house, that passed us by and was not ours. It was not in Damian's nature to halt an adventure that was already under way, not in his nature to acquire from nowhere the decency that would forbid it to proceed. His bedroom would not be empty when morning came, the small suitcase gone, a note left on his bedside table. 'Remember the others?' Claire whispered in the dark, and I knew whom she meant without having to think – the daughter of the Bishop of Killaloe, the widow from upstate New York, the Englishwoman in Venice, and other nameless women mentioned by our friend in passing.

Ill-suited, we said, when we learnt that the first of his marriages had fallen apart, and were too busy in those busy days to be more than sorry. We had hardly wondered about the fate of the bishop's daughter, and not at all about the American widow, except to say to one another that it was typical of Damian to make the same mistake twice. And when the Englishwoman left him it was a joke. Old reprobate, we said. Incorrigible.

The first streaks of dawn came flickering in, the birds began. We lay there silent, not trusting ourselves to comment on this past that the present had thrown up. The bishop's daughter – younger than

Joanna was now – smiled in her wedding dress, and I felt again the warm touch of her cheek when I kissed it, and heard her reply to my good wishes, her shy voice saying she was happier than she deserved to be. And a face from a photograph we'd once been shown was the oval face of the American, dark hair, dark eyes, lips slightly parted. And the face of the Englishwoman was just a guess, a face contorted in a quarrel, made bitter with cold tears. The shadows of other men's wives, of lovely women, girls charmed, clamoured for attention, breaking from their shadows, taking form. Old reprobate.

'I think I'll go and talk to her.' Claire's voice was hushed in the twilight, but she didn't move, and I knew that already she had changed her mind; talking would make everything worse. Eighty-one, Claire said: he would be eighty-one when Joanna was forty-eight.

I didn't calculate. It didn't matter. I thought we might quarrel, that tiredness might bring something like that on, but we didn't. We didn't round on each other, blaming in order to shed guilt, bickering as we might have once, when upsets engendered edginess. We didn't because ours are the dog days of marriage and there aren't enough left to waste: dangerous ground has long ago been charted and is avoided now. There was no point in saying, either, that the damage we already sensed would become entertainment for other people, as damage had for us.

'I'll make tea,' I said, and descended the stairs softly as I always do at this early hour so as not to wake our daughter. Some time today Damian and I might again call in at Traynor's; I might, in sickening humility, ask for mercy. I heard my own voice doing so, but the sound was false, wrong in all sorts of ways; I knew I wouldn't say a thing. To ensure that our daughter had a roof over her head I would lend whatever was necessary. A bungalow would replace the fallen house at Doul.

The *Irish Times* was half pushed through the letter-box; I slipped it out. I brought the tray back to our bedroom, with gingersnap biscuits on a plate because we like them in the early morning. We read the paper. We didn't say much else.

Later that morning Joanna hurried through cornflakes and a slice of toast. Her car started, reversed, then dashed away. Damian appeared and we sat outside in the September sunshine; Claire made fresh coffee. It was too late to hate him. It was too late to deny that we'd been grateful when our stay-at-home smugness had been enlivened by the tales of his adventures, or to ask him if he knew how life had turned out for the women who had loved him. Instead we conversed inconsequentially.

Published by Colophon Press in an edition of 207 copies
printed by letterpress on Zerkall mould-made paper

175 copies, numbered 1 – 175, are sewn into Murillo
card covers and signed by the author

26 copies, lettered A – Z, are bound in cloth and signed
by the author, and include a holograph
quotation from the text

6 copies, numbered I – VI, are for private distribution

This is copy    VI